Elena Marica

Something Called
Love

First published in Great Britain by Elena Marica

Copyright © Elena Marica 2017

The rights of Elena Marica to be identified as author of this work has been asserted in accordance with section 77 and 78 of the Copyright, Design and Patent Act 1988.

A CIP catalogue record for this book is available from the British Library.

ISBN: 978-0-9934402-3-6

A wonderful, heartwarming story to read by the fireplace during the holiday season.

Introduction

Many years have passed since Alyona lived in Siberia, in a town called Novosibirsk, where the snow was so heavy that when the winds blew, it drifted and swallowed the whole city. Even so, Alyona enjoyed those beautiful winter days. She remembered the huge snowflakes that fluttered down from the gray sky in bunches that clung to her eyelids, melting in seconds and dropping to her pink cheeks.

The day she left Novosibirsk, she thought her world had ended. Every Christmas day, she felt that something was missing. She watched families gather together, but she couldn't have that in her own life. She found a little consolation in spending time with friends and colleagues, but that wasn't enough to fill the emptiness in her soul. Everyone else had a family for Christmas, while hers had fallen apart years before. Memories of her teenage years flashed through her mind. She hadn't had an easy childhood, but she missed that time of her life so much.

For Alyona, nothing was more magical than the Christmas season. Christmas was the most beautiful time of the year, and she did everything in her power to celebrate the special day as best she could. However, she couldn't deny that the past 13 December 25ths had been the loneliest days of her life. This wasn't because of her relationship status; being single during the holiday season could sometimes be nice, as she didn't have to stress out about buying an expensive gift for a boyfriend. Certainly, Alyona would have been thrilled to have had a man in her life, but the thing she desired most was to spend Christmas with her mother. It was something she desperately missed.

To all of you who love Christmas as much as I do, I hope this book nurtures your soul and your heart, inspiring you to enjoy life and all it offers.

Chapter One

Leaving her childhood home broke her heart. Alyona thought she'd never be the same. She managed to harden her heart and stay away from emotional memories. She dedicated her life to her career—selling property. It was a hard job, but very rewarding. She'd learned to make money—a great deal of money. However, she lost something in the process, something more important than money. Her mother may not have loved Alyona the way she'd loved her sister, but Alyona still missed her every single day. She wondered whether her mother thought of her from time to time.

As she stepped off the train, snow was falling in the square, the snowflakes dancing madly in the sharp wind. The dark sky was the perfect backdrop for the whirling crystals. The snow covered the street and created a powdery white dusting on the rooftops and trees. It was like a scene from a greeting card. *Beautiful!* Alyona enjoyed the falling snow, which was whitening her long her. She walked along the street that would take her to her house. *God, it's so cold.* She could only imagine what those poor beggars outside were feeling. Her frozen hands struggled to open her bag. She leaned towards a poor man and threw some cash in his small box.

"Thank you! God bless you," the old man said.

"Have a good Christmas and try to keep warm," Alyona replied, giving him a warm smile.

The man took the money from the box and hid it inside the pocket of his large coat, which someone had probably gifted to him. This reminded Alyona that she needed to give away some of her old clothes, too. There were so many people in need this time of year and she had so many clothes that she never wore.

As she passed the corner pub, she almost walked into another man sitting next to the building. He must have been drunk. His shirt was pulled out of his trousers, but he didn't seem to care much. He was tightly gripping a red Santa hat, as if scared that someone would steal it. His other hand was busy holding a bottle to his mouth.

The man stared at her. "Hey, beautiful! Do you want to have a drink with me? You are so gorgeous. Let's get to know each other."

Alyona ignored him, though she wished someone would help him stand up and get home safely.

"Hey, where are you going? Talk to me!" The man continued to speak with no interruption.

Alyona walked ahead, continuing to ignore him. He must have had a lot to drink, because she could smell the alcohol on his breath.

"Hey! Come back! Why don't you talk to me?"

As Alyona walked faster, the man's words faded into the distance. After another hundred meters, she took the right-hand side and walked ahead to the road that led down to her house. As she walked, she observed the lights pouring out from the windows, piercing the veil of snow. She heard faint Christmas songs as she passed each window. Her own steps crunched in the snow. Then, suddenly, she heard another set of footsteps behind her. She sped up and turned her head to see who was following her, but it was almost impossible to see through the heavy snowflakes. She walked as fast as she could.

Eventually, she got to her gate and jumped inside, then quickly closed it behind her. She pulled back with both hands to make sure it was secure. She sighed and walked towards the house.

A man's hand grabbed the gate and stared at her in disbelief. "Hey... hey..."

Alyona turned and looked at him for a second. She had never seen the man before. She turned her head and walked away, ignoring him. Then she heard another voice speak.

"Excuse me. How can I help you, Sir?"

As she heard the other man speaking, curiosity made Alyona stop to hear what the stranger would say.

"Oh, thanks! God. I can't find the remote control."

"Do you live here, Sir?"

"Uh... yeah... I do live here. I just moved into one of the new flats." The man indicated with his hand.

"Really? I live there, too," the other man said.

"Alright, shall we open this gate, then? I'm freezing," the stranger said as rubbed his cold hands together.

The other man smiled, nodding. "You know, now I remember you. I saw you carrying boxes the other day."

"Yes, that was me. I'm Bradley Sno...."

"Nice to meet you! I'm Colin, flat 48," the other man interrupted. "Perhaps we can have a drink one of these days."

"Sure," Bradley said. "And thank you for saving me tonight. It's damn freezing outside."

Alyona stood behind a tree, listening to the conversation between the two men. She was freezing herself, but she smiled. How crazy she was to have left the poor man outside. But, as her friend Lexi said, a bit of prudence was always good.

For a moment, Alyona was tempted to laugh at the absurdity. She felt stupid. However, now she knew that she was safe. She entered her house, took a hot shower and bundled up in her pajamas and flannel robe. She put on her warm sleepers, then went into the kitchen and prepared a cup of hot chocolate with lots of cinnamon on top. She gazed out the window. It seemed to have been snowing forever. She breathed over the cold window, then leaned forward and rubbed the pane with her finger. After a few minutes, she stepped away and sat on the sofa by the open fire, her eyes fixed on the Christmas tree illuminating the room with its colorful lights. She watched Picky, her little dog, sleeping next to the fire. She felt lonely. The memory of her mother returned. *God knows how cold home can be this time of year.* Novosibirsk in the winter was bitterly cold. The Siberian city—the city of wind and snow. That was how she remembered it. The last time she had seen her city and her childhood home was thirteen years ago, before she had packed her stuff and left that place for good. She had felt that she didn't belong there, and the continuous arguments with her sister led Alyona to conclude that it would be better for everyone if she left. After all, London had given her so much. This could be the right place for her. She'd built her life here, and now she didn't want to live anywhere else. She sighed. She hadn't seen her mother for thirteen years. During this period, she had written nine letters, but had sent none of them. Now, whatever she was doing, whether walking her dog, shopping, sitting on the train, or reading the newspapers, the tenor of her thoughts was always the same: "How is my mother? Is she alive and well?" Alyona wanted to see her, but she didn't have the courage to confront her after all this time...

But now Christmas had arrived and Alyona could no longer endure the silence. She decided to write a new letter. She placed the cup on the sink, lowered the cooker fire, and sat at the table with a pen in her hand. "What shall I write?" She glanced around the kitchen; the pot of soup that was cooking began breathing out vapor. The kitchen was hot, so she opened the steamed-up window. Uh, uh, uh ...

"What shall I write?" she repeated.

"I'm writing this letter for love; I should know what to say." Then, she began. *"To my beloved mother Serafima, I am sending you greetings and love. I am alive and well, and I wish you a very Merry Christmas."* Alyona stopped to think. *"I hope you wish the same for me –"* She burst into tears. That was all she could write. She went to the window and stuck out her head. She took a deep breath. A few snowflakes fell on her face. She stayed there for a while.

That night, Alyona didn't sleep. She lay awake thinking that 10 letters could not contain all she wanted to say to her mother. Since she had left, she had felt as lonely as an orphan. How many things had happened in her life throughout all these years... how hard her days were and how long the nights had been. She reflected for a moment. Thirteen years was a long time. Maybe her mother was no longer alive. She checked the clock again; it was 3 a.m. She stood up, put on her warm gown and went back into the kitchen. She took the paper and began to write swiftly.

Dear Mother,

"An occurrence has separated us..." Alyona's lips moved and she spoke in a low voice.

"I should like to see you! But perhaps you don't want me to...." She wanted to tell her mother how much she missed her, but could not find the words to express it. For long minutes, she sat with her legs crossed under the table. Then the pen began to scratch, drawing long, curly lines across the paper. She wrote at full speed and often underlined sentences with double lines. Suddenly, her mind was clear

and her eyes looked at the words with confidence. She wrote a few pages, and once she finished, she read them aloud from beginning to end. It was the most beautiful letter she had ever written. Alyona put the pages into an envelope and went back to bed. She lay awake, full of restless thoughts.

The next morning, she walked to the post office to post the letter to her mother. It was the 23th of December and the post office was open as usual; the only difference was that the workers were wearing special uniforms wishing everyone a merry Christmas. Alyona sent the letter by express delivery. She took a deep breath, hoping that her mother would receive it in three days, perhaps four. She took her leather gloves from her pocket, then put them on and walked out of the post office, intending to do some shopping on her way home.

Chapter Two

Alyona looked up into the whirl of falling snowflakes, trying to focus on just one.

"I'm sorry, Miss." A man pushed her slightly, then stepped inside the gate and closed it behind him, ignoring Alyona's intention of getting inside, too.

"Excuse me!" Alyona called.

The man ignored her.

"Excuse me!" Alyona insisted.

"Yes, how may I help you, Miss?"

"I live here too. Would you please let me in?" Alyona said.

"Oh, I'm sorry Miss, but I don't know you."

"Well, I don't know you either," Alyona said, frustrated and upset at having left the remote control on her kitchen table.

"Well, how can I let you in if I don't know who you're? You could be that type of girl who wants to get into her ex-boyfriend's flat and kill him because he cheated on her with her best friend," he said, trying to maintain his serious demeanor, though he looked amused.

"I can't believe this! Do I look like that kind of person?"

"Well, you don't look happy," he replied, smiling.

"Alright, that's fine. Don't worry about the gate," she said. Alyona began ringing the other flats, but nobody was home. She stepped away, deciding to go for a walk; eventually, someone would come back home and open the gate for her.

"Wait, wait... I was just joking. I can open the gate for you."

"Is this some kind of game you're playing?" Alyona breathed out. She looked up at the man. He was tall, with dark brown hair, stylishly cropped, falling over his ocean green eyes. A broad smile was spread across his face, revealing his immaculate white teeth.

He elegantly held the gate and Alyona walked in.

"I'm sorry for that. I thought it was funny. I'm Bradley. And you are?" He extended his hand.

"It wasn't funny at all. And you don't need to know my name." *Thanks anyway, though.*

"Uh... did I really upset you?"

"That was a silly joke," Alyona said, then walked away.

"Wait! Wait! I'm sorry, I didn't mean to upset you." Bradley ran behind her.

"It's okay."

"No, it's not okay. I can clearly see you're upset. Can I do anything to make you forgive my stupid joke?"

"It's fine. You don't need to follow me..."

"I don't. I just don't want you to be upset with me."

"And why would you care about that? You don't know me, right?"

"Well, because we're neighbors, and I don't want you to be upset with me."

"It's all right, trust me. I'm just one of many neighbors."

"You really fit the role of the perfect single, don't you?"

Alyona shook her head. For a fleeting moment, she didn't know whether to take the remark as a sarcastic classification of her current status, or as an innocent compliment.

"So, can we be friends? What do you think?" he asked.

"I think neighbors sounds better," Alyona replied.

"I want you to forgive me for this small incident. Would you accept having dinner with me?"

Alyona watched him, surprised by his proposal. His eyes were fixed on her, searching for an answer.

"I'm sorry, I can't have dinner with you."

"Lunch, tomorrow?" Bradley smiled. "If you don't have any other plans..."

"I do have other plans!"

"Of course you do. What am I thinking? You must have so many invitations." He glanced at her. Alyona was a very pretty girl, tall, with long brown hair tied back into a ponytail. She wore a dark jacket over a white shirt. Long boots covered jeans that showed the shape of her perfect legs. Bradley was lost in a reverie for a moment, tempted to grab her and kiss her. He half-wished she felt the same.

"I'd really like to have lunch with you, if you change your plans," Bradley insisted.

Alyona gazed around for few seconds, her eyes wide and brown, her pink lips pursed in thought. "I'll have to think about it."

"Great, thank you. This is my number. Let me know what time you want to meet." He handed her a card and expected hers, but she didn't reciprocate.

"I said I'll think about it. This doesn't mean the answer is yes."

"Well, I hope it's yes. You still haven't told me your name, though."

"Alyona."

"Alyona, I'll be waiting for your call!"

"I can't guarantee I'll…" she replied, then walked away. *How did he know I'm single? Is it written on my face?*

Finding herself single at 35 was the last thing she'd expected. *Having a great career makes me happy. But apart from that, what do I have? Nothing, nothing … I'm not even dating anyone.*

As she walked up the stairs, she heard the dog scratching on the door. *Thank God I've got you.* She opened the door and her expression softened. She saw the dog with his big eyes, waiting for her prompt at the door.

"Hey!" She started to cuddle the dog as he jumped in her arms and stretched his neck to smell the box in her other hand.

"Do you want a piece of cake? I don't think that would be healthy for you, though. It's a bit different from the food you eat. And your stomach is quite sensible when it comes to sweets. Better get your food ready. What do you think?" She placed the white box in the fridge and went to prepare his food. The dog walked behind her, playing around her feet. "What is it? Did you miss me? Here you go." She set down the plate, and the dog started to eat hungrily.

Alyona turned on the stereo. She put on classic music and began to sing along. She felt good. Why on the earth should she be so anxious to have a boyfriend? She had been there before, and she had been heartbroken more than once. She didn't need that pain again. Maybe she'd want to settle down one day, but she still had a lot of living to do.

Chapter Three

The next morning, after Christmas, Alyona decided to call her old friend Nick with the intention of wishing him the compliments of the season.

Nick was lounging on the sofa in a blue dressing gown, a pile of crumpled morning papers around him. Beside the couch was his dog, staring at him and barking, annoyed, from time to time.

"You're occupied," said Alyona. "Perhaps I interrupted you."

"Not at all," Nick replied, as bored as his dog. "I'm glad to have a friend with whom I can talk on Christmas Day." That was a clue reminding her that she should have called him the day before.

"Nick, I know I should have called you before. I'm sorry. As you know, I was invited to my boss's house to spend Christmas Day."

"I know, you were too busy to remember an old friend."

"Don't say that! It's just one day, you can't punish me for that!"

"No, no. No crime," said Nick, laughing. "Only one request; please don't spend New Year's Eve with him, too."

"I'm not planning that at all!" Alyona laughed.

"Well, knowing your boss, any possible combination of events may be expected to take place, my dear. I observed that lately you're spending a lot of time with him, more than with your friends."

"It's just work, I assure you. I've already had experience with such..."

"I hope you're right and that this matter won't fall into the same category," Nick said.

"I know what I'm doing. I just want to prove to him that I'm good enough for that promotion."

"I hope you're right. Don't fall for him in the meantime." Nick somehow felt jealous.

"I won't allow that to happen. I won't be anyone's trophy."

"Well, my dear, stay with me. I'll never treat you like a trophy. I promise." Nick laughed.

Alyona laughed, too. She loved Nick's sarcasm. Since his wife had left him, he had shown a preference for men. That didn't bother her. Nick had always been her good friend. She remembered, five months after his divorce, Nick had introduced her to his new love, a young, skinny guy. At first, Alyona thought it was a joke. However, watching the two of them together, she realized that Nick was serious. *Was he really becoming gay? Or deep inside, had he always been?*

"You always had different tastes, Nick!" Alyona said.

"And I don't regret it, my dear. I'm happy with my life the way it is."

"I'm sure you are, Nick."

Nick was calm person who led a sedentary life, got out little, was out of training entirely. He was middle-aged, with grizzled hair which he covered with styling cream.

His character may have accounted for the fact that his wife had ceased to love him and had left him after just a few years of marriage.

Nick was a very intellectual man. It was the first thing that had caught Alyona's attention when she had met him at her friend's wedding. She knew a man like Nick, with such a large brain, must have something in it. Nick was a big man with sizable shoulders and a broad, intelligent face, sloping down to a pointed beard of dark brown. When he gave the speech at the wedding, everybody paused with opened mouths. Nick chose his words with care; his voice was profoundly deep, and he gave the impression of an educated man from high society.

Nick and Alyona had sat at the same table. Alyona liked socializing; even after 4 years in London, she felt like she was still new to this place and she needed to make contacts.

When Nick had told her about his friend, a woman who owned a real estate agency and who was looking for people to hire, Alyona was excited.

Nick introduced her to his friend, and that was how Alyona got her first job in real estate. After that, slowly, Nick and Alyona became good friends. Nick continued helping her with advice about jobs, and about her private life, too.

"Did your friend from Paris come to visit you?" Alyona asked Nick.

"No, he missed the flight. So, I celebrated Christmas with my dog. We had a beer with a burger and some fries." Nick glanced at his dog. "Sorry I couldn't give you any; there wasn't enough beer for myself."

"That's what you have every single day, Nick," Alyona said. "You should have ordered something different. It was Christmas Day, for God's sake."

"Nah, and who cares about Christmas anyway? Are you coming to visit me today?"

"No, not today. I'm just passing through the markets for the last shopping, then heading back home. My dog is waiting for his walk."

Nick laughed.

"What was that?" Alyona asked.

"Ideally, you'd be going for a walk with a man, not with your dog." Nick didn't like the idea of her being single.

"Nick, you must know me by now. I'm tired of ending up in the wrong relationships and then getting hurt."

"You need to change that, my dear. Concentrate on finding the right one. Life doesn't last forever."

"I don't believe in that anymore."

"C'mon, don't give me that. Everybody dreams about a romantic love."

Alyona rolled her eyes. Nick was the type of man who saw romance and happily-ever- after in every relationship, though not his own. Alyona figured out that Nick fancied her boss, but she didn't want to encourage him. The relationship between the two men had nothing to do with romance, but Nick liked to play with the idea, hoping that her boss would change his mind about women and think about crossing to the other side. Nick would be happy to show him the new life ... and would make sure the relationship between the two of them worked.

******

I should make more time for myself too. Somehow Alyona admitted the fact that she was too busy with her job to have time for a social life. After her last relationship that broke her heart, she dated occasionally, but she hadn't found anyone to make her heart race again. Bil Welson, the man she'd been seeing lately, was more of a friend than a love interest.

And after a few dates with Dave, she was a bit hesitant to get involved again...

* * * * * *

Back home, Alyona set down the heavy shopping bags and sighed with relief. This was it. She was done with the shopping for this year. Now, she would take Picky, her dog, outside and then, once she was back, she'd cook some ginger biscuits. She sighed, as this thought reminded her of her mother. *She may be receiving my letter soon.*

Alyona picked up her key and made her way downstairs. The dog followed her with small steps. "C'mon, c'mon, let's go!" She began running and playing with the dog. Picky was a loving dog, intelligent and mischievous, but at the same time goofy and playful. However, just as he was smart enough to learn good habits, he was smart enough to learn the bad ones. Alyona had to train him often. As they made their way across to the park, Picky paused for few seconds. He began to smell the footprints over the white snow, then followed the path until he bumped into a stranger's shoe. Picky raised his head and, with his big black eyes, looked at the stranger in silence.

"Picky, come back here!" Alyona called.

Picky didn't care about his owner; he began playing around the stranger's feet.

"Picky, come here!" Alyona called again. She couldn't understand her dog's behavior. Picky usually had a hard time meeting strangers.

"I'm sorry, I've never seen my dog doing this before." Alyona bent to pick up her dog.

"They say a dog can recognize a good-hearted person, and it seems that this dog likes me already. I just need to convince his owner to like me too," the man said.

"Excuse me!" Alyona glanced at the man, whose hat was almost covering his eyes. She paused, surprised. He was very good looking ... too good looking. Tall with a built body, perhaps in his early 40s, wise and mature. Alyona met his eyes and it seemed as though she knew him immediately.

Her crooked smile told him she'd read his thoughts perfectly. He pulled up his hat.

"Bradley?"

"Hi. You never called."

"Hi. I ... I wanted to, but..."

"But?"

"I've been tremendously busy lately." Alyona didn't know what other excuses to give. She felt uncomfortable and realized that Bradley was staring at her breasts. Not openly, but she caught him looking. She suddenly felt cold and looked down. Well, no wonder; her coat had somehow come undone and her shirt had fallen open a few buttons down. She quickly pulled her coat together at the throat and managed to close the buttons with one hand. "It's a bit cold today," she said.

"Yes, it is." Bradley took off his expensive scarf and wrapped it around her neck. "Take this. It'll help you stay warm," he said.

Alyona could feel his hot breath on her neck as he put his scarf around her.

Bradley gazed at her and smiled. For a moment she thought he was going to kiss her.

"It fits you very well," he said.

Alyona watched him staring at her. He was handsome, six-foot-tall, with an athletic body and beautiful eyes.

The encounter left Alyona dazed. If someone had told her a few days ago that Bradley, her arrogant neighbor, would have this impact on her, she would have laughed her head off.

Chapter Four

B radley... What an enigma he was. She had seen him just twice. She knew hardly anything about him, other than his name and his address. Okay, he was also very good-looking, seemed honest, and her dog liked him—which was curious. And, of course, his dog and hers had become friends already. However, not knowing anything else about Bradley felt like a forbidden bite with a constant itch. Alyona began to fantasize. *I don't know where he comes from – from another world, perhaps. And yet, I've never felt this way about another man before. Is this a gift that was sent to me?* One thing was certain. Alyona wanted to discover more about who Bradley really was. It seemed he didn't like to speak about himself, either. She had to face the fact that she liked him... after all, it was the time of year when miracles could happen.

Alyona glanced at the watch. It was almost 7 p.m.; Bradley would be there soon. She had accepted his invitation for dinner.

After a few minutes, the doorbell rang and Alyona opened the door. Bradley looked even better than he had that morning.

"Hi."

"Hi." He sat on the doorstep, his brilliant eyes watching her. He was a man of genuine intention – they were hard to find in the real world.

"Come in!" Alyona said in her low, pleasant voice.

"I brought this for you. I hope you like them," Bradley said as he gave her a bouquet of red roses and an elegant box of chocolates.

"They're beautiful. Thank you, but you shouldn't...."

"Yes, I should," Bradley interrupted, then out of the blue he kissed her cheek.

Alyona blushed at the gesture.

Bradley entered the living room, where Picky jumped, licking and playing around his new shoes.

"It's obvious he likes you," Alyona said.

"Hey buddy," Bradley caressed his head, and Picky went mad.

"I'll take my coat and then we're ready to go." Alyona was astonished at the sight of the two of them playing. She couldn't explain what Bradley's secret was, why the dog got mad when he saw Bradley.

******

They reached the restaurant. Alyona and Bradley took their places at a small table at the end of the restaurant, next to a fireplace. The waiter handed them menus. It was a cozy place. The flames danced in sync with the relaxing songs, illuminating Alyona's face, revealing its splendor and beauty. Once they ordered their food, Bradley turned to Alyona and invited her to dance with him.

Alyona gazed around the restaurant. Their table was far from the others; it seemed Bradley had booked this corner for just the two of them...

Bradley extended his hand and, without waiting for an answer, helped her stand. He curled his arm around her waist. The song was incredibly romantic. Bradley stroked her hair with his hand and gently kissed her head. "I think I've searched for you forever."

Alyona murmured something; she didn't know how to reply to that. It was a declaration she hadn't expected, though her thoughts were the same.

Bradley pinned her with his eyes. "Did you say something?"

"No, I didn't," Alyona replied.

Suddenly, Bradley felt confused and let down. Maybe she didn't share his feelings. How strange. He was sure Alyona had given him a different signal when they met in the park. *Is she playing hard to get?* Because, if so, this intrigued him even more.

"You're a good dancer!" he said.

Alyona lifted her face with a composed expression. "And you, too." She smiled, and her face brightened. Her red lips and brown eyes made her irresistible.

Bradley gave her a teasing smile. "I think our food is ready. Shall we?"

"Sure."

Bradley led her to the table, held the chair, and stepped back to let her sit.

"Thank you!"

"My pleasure," he said, then sat at the table. They began to eat their meal. After a while, he decided to ask her the question. "Any plans for New Year's Eve?"

"I have a few options, but I haven't decided which one to go for." She sipped her red wine, sneaking a few glances at him. "What about you? Are you going away from London?"

"I was hoping to go home this year, but due to the circumstances I don't think that will happen."

"Let me guess. Your wife threw you out of the house?" Alyona tossed out the question. She wanted to know if single, married, was divorced, widowed..."

"How could you tell?"

"Well, you don't like to talk much about yourself, so I assume you're..."

"You don't like to talk much about yourself, either. You may have a husband and kids somewhere." Bradley burst out laughing.

"What do you mean?"

"Nothing, I was just assuming."

"This is ridiculous. Do you mind if I finish eating my salmon before it gets cold?"

"Please, eat." He leaned forward a little. "There will be plenty of other nights out to discover each other's lives." He smiled.

Alyona smiled back. It was exactly what she wanted to hear.

"Where is home for you?" she asked.

"Somewhere in North England. However, if you change your plans, maybe we can spend New Year's Eve together?" he suggested.

"I can't promise anything."

"Sure. I mean, I'd be happy if you changed your plans." Bradley smiled, intrigued at the turn of events in his life. It was the first time he had spent Christmas vacation alone. Since he broke up with Jessica, he had to move and change phone numbers. His ex-girlfriend couldn't accept the idea that their relationship had come to an end. She had practically been stalking him. Alyona seemed so different. Well, he had met her just a few times, it was early to say, but it felt so right.

They spent the night laughing and dancing. After dinner, Bradley offered his hand as they walk home. They held hands for a few seconds, and then Alyona pulled away. Bradley gazed in her eyes. She could see that he wanted to touch her again. The odd thing was, she wanted that too, but at the same time she felt silly about her feelings. She didn't even know him. But still, his broad smile was hard to resist. Oh God. She could easily fall into a passionate love affair with him.

They sat outside her house and Bradley moved a step forward so he could be closer. "I can't believe someone so absolutely beautiful is single."

Alyona blushed.

"All the man in the restaurant were staring at you," he continued. "But lucky me, I had the chance to have dinner with you." He bent to her ear and whispered, "I'm not married. You're a terrible guesser."

Alyona tried hard not to smile. Bradley leaned forward slowly. Alyona watched him, mesmerized with his ocean green eyes. Bradley's hand slowly touched her face, then held her head. Alyona didn't lean closer, but she didn't pull away either. Without Alyona realizing it, her eyes closed and their lips met. She felt her body melt into the most romantic and seductive kiss. She arched her arms around his neck and slowly moved her body into his, closer and closer, wanting more. He made a little noise of pleasure. Their kiss went on and on. Bradley was the first man Alyona had kissed after her ex-boyfriend and she wanted to enjoy every second of it. She moaned, wrapped her arms around him, and slowly pushed her breast over his chest. He felt the tremor in her body. He wanted to enjoy it all; he couldn't resist. Their kiss was mind-blowing. His body felt like it was on fire, ready to explode, which shock the hell out of him.

Alyona suddenly stopped. She took a deep breath, looking at him in astonishment. Before he realized what was going on, Alyona slid out of his arms. "I ... um... I should get to bed. It must be very late." Then she hurried away, leaving him without words.

Bradley sat there for long minutes. *What is it about you, Alyona, that drives me mad?*

I want to learn all about you.

Chapter Five

Alyona sat at the table and patiently awaited the arrival of her cappuccino. She glanced at her watch. It was 9:10 a.m. A tiny blonde girl with round glasses and a red apron placed the large cup of cappuccino on the table along with a plate containing a variety of biscuits. Alyona carried the cup to her mouth and almost burned her tongue as a voice broke into the silent moment.

"Hey..."

"Hey, I didn't expect you to come."

"I'll never miss breakfast with the most beautiful girl I know," Nick said.

"Your lateness is forgiven." Alyona smiled.

"I guess I always know the right thing to say."

"I guess you're right." Alyona nodded, knowing that would make Nick happy.

"You agree with me for once."

"I do."

"Thanks," Nick replied, relieved. "I could see something different in you today. Are these the eyes of a woman in love?" He glanced at her, waiting for an answer.

Alyona burst into laughter. "What are you saying?"

"I'm saying you look different today. And you can't lie to me because I know you very well."

For a moment, Alyona wanted to deny, but she couldn't. Nick was staring at her, burning with curiosity. He knew precisely what was going on in her brain.

"You met someone... I can tell...." Nick sang out.

"Shhh..." Alyona moved forward slightly.

"So, you did?"

"Well, kinda."

"Who is it? Does this man have a name?"

"His name is Bradley. You won't believe it, but he's my neighbor."

"Hold on. Is that the old man who's sending flowers to your door every Sunday morning?"

"Noooo ... What are you saying?"

"Oh, thank God it's not him. I can't compete with him." Nick burst into laughter.

"That's not even funny. Alec is a really nice old man."

"So, who is this Bradley?"

"His full name is Bradley Snowdon. He's an investment banker."

"Hmmm... it seems this Bradley stole your heart."

"Oh... no, absolutely not. I mean, he's a nice guy, but we've just met."

"I believe it's more than just nice. I can see the spark in your eyes when you speak about him. You're falling for him, my dear."

"I don't think that's the reason why I'm happy."

"I think that's exactly the reason, my dear. And you have to honest with yourself for once."

"Well, I admit it, I like him in a way. His funny and charming. He makes me laugh, and I feel happy around him."

"That's what you deserve. I'm thrilled for you. And I hope he treats you well. Otherwise, he'll have to deal with me."

Alyona smiled; she appreciated Nick's over-protection. They had been friends for more than 8 years and Nick was the only person who had been at her side when she needed a shoulder to cry on. She glanced at him enjoying his espresso.

"You think I'm joking!" Nick wiped his mouth with a paper towel.

"I know you mean it, Nick. But I'm fine. I have the feeling this time it's different." Alyona couldn't allow Nick to get upset about some-thing that hadn't happened—although a bit of precaution didn't hurt.

"I need to get a gift for my mother." Nick suddenly changed the subject. "Do you think you can help me with that?"

"I don't have plans today. We can go shop-ping after we finish here."

"Wonderful. I'm going to pay the bill and then we're ready to go."

"Alright," Alyona said. "I'm going to get the car from the parking lot. I'll pick you up outside, at the bar entrance."

"Okay, but don't run away," Nick said.

"I'll come to pick you up, Nick. Stay at the door." Alyona wanted a few minutes to herself to call Bradley. He had called her earlier, but she was driving and couldn't pick up the phone. She punched in his number, but the phone went straight to voice mail. She tried again, with no luck. She decided she'd call him later. *Why did he switch off the phone? Is he seeing someone else?* Alyona couldn't hide the fact that he was on her mind every minute. She felt the cold wind blowing her hair and she hurried. With a click of her key-chain, she unlocked the car and opened the door, then threw the bag on the backseat. She drove towards the bar and Nick jumped inside.

"Oh, how lovely. I feel so much better now. It's freezing outside." Nick rubbed his hands.

"Yes, it is." Alyona nodded. A melody flipped over the radio, and she held her breath as she remembered her dinner with Bradley.

"It looks like my mother's favorite shop is open today," Nick said.

"Great! Let's park the car." Alyona's phone rang and she reached for her bag to retrieve it. *That must be Bradley, finally. He must have seen my calls...*

She picked up the phone. The number displayed on it was that of her boss's office. He was probably asking her about some paperwork. The office was closed until after the New Year; what was he doing there. This would be the first time in five years that Alyona was off for the whole season.

"Do you want me to come into the office now?" she asked, glancing at Nick and shrugging her shoulders.

"No, since you're on holiday, I couldn't ask you to do that. It's not necessary, I can sort this out myself."

"Fabulous! Then if that's settled, I can get on with my day. I have a few things to do. Plus, Nick and I are driving in the city. You remember Nick, don't you?"

"Of course." Malcolm, her boss, wasn't happy about what he heard, but he couldn't show her his insecurity. On the other hand, Alyona had never shown interest in him. Despite his irritation, he managed a weak smile. "All right," he muttered, "enjoy your day."

"Oh, thanks Malcolm. It'll be great fun," Alyona said ended the call.

"Wonderful." A smile lit up Nick's face. "Malcolm needs to learn to do things on his own. He can't call you whenever he wants."

"That's exactly what I'm trying to teach him." Alyona nodded.

"You're one of the best directors at his company, but that doesn't give him the right to control your life."

"Don't you worry about that; I can control his money instead," Alyona replied. They both burst out laughing.

Then, suddenly, Alyona stopped, puzzled. The man in the car beside her was staring at her, his eyes appearing shocked. Numb and speechless, Alyona turned to Nick, gesturing at him to stop, but Nick didn't understand what she was doing and continued laughing even louder. She turned, lowering the window, but the car next to her slipped away. Her pulse thundered like crazy.

"What is it?" Nick spoke over her shoulder, searching for a better view of the other car.

"The man in the other car was Bradley," Alyona replied, beating the wheel. "Now that he saw me with you, he may think I was playing with his feelings."

"Why do you think that?"

"What do you think? He just saw me in the car laughing and having fun with another man."

"We're just friends, for God's sake! We can have a laugh, right?"

"I know, but he doesn't know that."

"Well, you should call him and explain."

"I can't do this by phone. I need to talk to him personally. Now let's go and get that gift for your mother."

"Are you sure you still want to come with me?"

"Of course, don't be silly." She parked the car and reached for her bag. She was sure Bradley would be fine once she explained that Nick was just a friend.

Chapter Six

The next morning the doorbell chimed, and Alyona rolled onto her stomach. She entered the hallway full of energy and spirit. She looked at herself in the mirror and adjusted her hair, as it had formed a few curls overnight. *I'm sure this is Bradley. Thank God he decided to come over; I couldn't handle the embarrassment of knocking on his door.*

"Are you Alyona Sokolov?" the man asked.

"Yes, that's me."

"I have a delivery for you," he said.

"Ah, great." The online shop had dispatched her dress faster than she expected.

She signed, glancing at the man. "Is there anything else for me? A letter?"

"No, Miss, there's no letter, just this box."

"Thank you," she said lowering her face in sadness. She had hoped for a reply to the letter she had sent to her mother. Probably her mother would never write back. Alyona's decision to leave Novosibirsk had upset her mother very much. *"If you go now, don't ever come back."* They were tough words, but Alyona had been more or less forced to leave. And Masha, her older sister, had done everything to get Alyona out of her way.

Sad and frustrated, Alyona went inside and lay back on the bed, closing her eyes. It was possible that her mother hadn't forgiven her, after all these years.

As though he felt her sadness, Picky jumped into the bed and placed his head on her.

Alyona caressed his head. "Hey, do you want to go for a walk?"

Picky's eyes brightened in excitement, and he ran to the door impatiently.

"Okay, okay, can you hold it a bit? I'm getting ready."

It didn't take her more than a few minutes to put something on. As she opened the door, Picky ran down the stairs.

"Oh, darling, I'm sorry I kept you inside for so long." She opened the main door and Picky ran into the garden.

Outside, it wasn't very cold. The sun shone over the immaculate snow. The garden looked like a fairy-tale world. The trees were adorned with thick pillows of white, the ground was a smooth blanket. In the middle was a man with two kids. They had already finished a snowman and they looked very happy with their master-piece. They clothed him with a red scarf and hat.

"I think this will keep him warm, Father," the child with the green jacket said.

"It's snowing, Father!" said the other boy, excited.

"No, it's not!" his brother replied.

"Father, look, it's snowing!" The boy grabbed his father's hand.

Alyona felt something rubbing against her face. She looked to the sky, which had suddenly turned gray. She felt something soft and cold falling over her skin; then she saw the snow-flakes falling through the air. In the garden, there was about three inches of snow, and it was still coming down. The two boys started throwing snowballs, running and horsing around the snowman. Their father joined them; he looked very childish, but they were all happy enjoying the snow.

Alyona smiled; she felt the happiness in the air, too. She took a breath and decided she needed to speak with Bradley. She would go to his house later. She had to explain yesterday's incident to him. She wanted to let him know that Nick was a very good friend and there was nothing between them. Lost in her thoughts, she watched her dog walking about. Then, as she looked to her other side, she saw a man staring at her. It was Bradley. She felt butterflies in her stomach. How long had he been staring at her? He was so fine-looking in his new dark blue coat. He was always dressed impeccably—with expensive taste. His custom-tailored suit was beautiful. She guessed he was going to some important business meeting. She looked down at herself and felt a bit embarrassed about her casual clothes. The eye contact between the two of them lasted for what seemed like long minutes. Alyona smiled at him, but he didn't return her smile. His gaze lingered on her long enough to make her conscious that something bothered him. He looked at her as if he expected something. He stepped forward as if he wanted to say something, but then he turned away. At first, she thought he was walking toward her to kiss her; then she thought he wasn't, which make her feel stupid.

"Bradley!" she called.

"Yes." He turned halfway around.

"Wait, I need to talk to you."

Bradley hesitated for a second, then stopped.

"Bradley, before you say anything, I want to explain to you about the man you saw in my car yesterday."

"You don't need to explain yourself. You're free to do what you want with your life."

"No, it's not what you think. The man you saw yesterday is my best friend. There's absolutely nothing between me and him."

"Say what you want, but I know what I saw, and the way he was looking at you says more than your words."

Alyona struggled to hide a smile. Was he jealous of Nick?

"What's so funny?" Bradley asked.

"Look, Nick is my best friend, but he's not really the type of man I'd fall for. I'm sure if you met him, you'd understand why."

"I don't believe what you're saying. I saw how much fun you two had together," Bradley said.

"We were just laughing. Nothing else."

"Ah, of course. What else you could say? Look, I don't have time to listen to this," he said.

"Bradley, please don't say that. Nick is..."

"What? Is he your boyfriend?"

Alyona watched Bradley as seriously as she could, but in the end, she couldn't hide her amusement.

"I make you laugh, huh? I feel like an idiot, thinking you were different from other women. Goodbye, Alyona," he said, stepping away.

"No, Bradley, wait! You're completely wrong. I have the same feelings about you. Our encounter meant a lot to me. You can't give up just because I have a male friend."

Bradley turned again. "I don't believe in male friends."

"Bradley, stop, please. Nick is gay! He's gay!"

"What? What did you say?" Bradley stopped.

"I said that Nick is gay! There's nothing between us. We're just friends."

Bradley looked at her, astonished. He felt stupid. He looked at Alyona blankly. "Are you kidding me?"

"No, this is the pure true. I didn't want to tell you that my best friend is gay."

"I feel so stupid."

"You aren't. How could you know?"

Bradley was speechless. Alyona held his gaze and gave him a sweet smile. Bradley watched her and finally smiled. She was so beautiful, and without makeup she was even more attractive. To make things even worse, she knew exactly what impact she could have on a man. She was the type of girl who attracted every man who passed by.

"I'm sorry," Bradley said.

"That's okay. You're forgiven." Alyona smiled.

"I have a proposition to make."

"Right here in the garden? We can go inside, to my house," Alyona said.

"No, here is good, as I don't have much time."

"Okay, go on."

"As we know, we're both single and we don't have big plans for New Year's Eve. I'm thinking we can do something together. I'm proposing a few days in Austria. There's a beautiful wooden chalet over there we can rent."

Alyona looked at him in astonishment. "In Austria?"

"Yes, in Austria. You have a couple of days to think about it," he said.

"Well, I still don't know you very well," Alyona replied.

"That's not a problem. This is an occasion to get to know me better."

Alyona shook her head. "How do I know you're not a serial killer?"

Bradley laughed. "You don't, but you can ask my ex. Oops, but she's already dead."

"What?"

"I'm just kidding. Never killed anybody—yet. You could be the first, though." He laughed.

"You're crazy."

"I think you're right. I'm crazy about you!"

Alyona shook her head, not sure what to say.

"Look, I know my proposal sounds crazy, but it's what I feel now. Please, would you at least consider it?"

Alyona looked at him for a moment, then said, "All right, I'll think about it."

"I'm leaving London in a few hours, but I'll be back tomorrow night." He leaned in and kissed her lips.

"Have a nice trip, wherever you're going." She desperately wanted to ask where he was going, but she didn't have the courage.

"I eagerly wait for your response." He stroked her hair with his hand and kissed her again, this time passionately.

Alyona felt the blood rising in her body.

"Wait for me." He turned and walked away.

Alyona stood still. This would be the first time she would blindly follow her instincts.

Chapter Seven

The man gave Masha a yellow envelope and asked her to sign her name to confirm the delivery. When the postman's footsteps had died away, Masha opened the envelope. Inside she found a letter addressed to her mother. She opened it, read a few lines, and then, still looking at the envelope, sauntered toward the little room where her mother was lying in a small bed.

Her mother was just 73 years old, but her body was in so much pain, she couldn't walk any longer. The years hadn't been kind to her. Masha entered the little room and handed the letter to her mother, saying, "This must be from Alyona." Then she left without raising her eyes.

Masha stopped not far from the door. She heard her mother reading the first lines in a trembling voice. She could go no further, but these were enough. Tears streamed from her eyes. "This is from my daughter," she cried. "She's in London!" Oh, oh! Holy Saints!

As she listened to her mother, Masha remembered back to when she had met an old friend of her sister's and asked whether she had heard from Alyona lately. However, the memories of the two sisters arguing had always interfered and the secret had remained looked within Masha. The fact was, Alyona had always been the competition and Masha had always been the one who lost. When Alyona had left, Masha couldn't stay in her skin. The memories of that last Christmas morning had never left Masha's mind. Her mother had bought Alyona a winter hat. It was a very ordinary red hat of the usual round shape, rough and much the worse for wear. However, it suited Alyona's pretty face very well. Masha took the hat in her hands and turned it over, rather upset.

"I think Mum intended to say that this hat is mine!"

"No, it's not! My name was written on the Christmas card," Alyona replied.

"No, it wasn't! You're lying."

"I'm not lying. The hat is mine." Alyona moved to grab the hat from Masha's hands.

Masha didn't let go; she held the hat with all her strength. Alyona pulled harder and Masha fall backwards, hitting her head on the furniture behind her. She began to scream and cry.

"Give me the hat!"

Her mother heard the screams and went into the room to check on what had happened.

"Mother, help! Alyona beat me up just because I wanted to try on the hat." Masha cried louder, holding her head to make the situation seem even more grave than it was. "Alyona, what have you done to your sister? Look at her head. You could have killed her. You're such a bad girl. I'm fed up with your behavior."

"I haven't touched her, Mother. She fell over by herself. I didn't touch her. I swear!" "Stupid girl! You ruin everything! Give me this hat—you don't deserve it!"

"But Mother, I need this hat. It's cold outside, and my old one is torn; it doesn't keep me warm enough."

"You'll have to use that one until next year."
Serafima took the hat from Alyona's hands and
gave it to her sister. "This is your hat now."

Alyona's face dropped and tears ran down
her cheeks. This was another piece of evidence
that her mother didn't love her. That was clear
enough. Alyona stepped away sadly. She didn't
want to see her mother and Masha hugging
each other. Seeing Alyona leave, Masha felt
very happy. However, what Masha couldn't imagine was that at that precise moment Alyona
made a promise to herself to leave that house.
It was obvious no one wanted her there.

******

"Masha! Masha!" Serafima called as loud
as she could. *Oh, my poor girl. How much she*

has suffered. Serafima cried out as memories flushed through her mind.

"Masha! Come here! I need to talk to you!"

"Mother, are you okay?" Masha asked as she entered the room.

"I've never been better. I want you to do me a favor."

"Yes, Mother. What is it?"

"I need you to write a letter to Alyona. Tell her to come home for Christmas."

"Oh, Mother, I know you want to see her, but she may not receive the letter in time for Christmas."

"You think so? Alright, you need to call her, then. Look, she wrote her number at the bottom of the letter." Her mother indicated with her finger.

"Um … I think a letter would be better," Masha suggested.

"You silly girl. You still hate her, don't you?"

"No, Mother, I don't hate her."

"Of course you do. I can see that in your eyes. Call Alyona and tell her to come home.

I want to see my daughter before I die."

Masha was aware of her mother's illness, and she couldn't deny her last wishes. But the thought of hearing Alyona's voice after all these years put her under stress.

"Masha! Look at me. Promise me you'll call Alyona."

"I promise, Mother," Masha said, unsure she could keep her word.

"Tell her to come as soon as she can. I hope she can forgive me for all I've done. My poor little girl. I threw her out of the home." A river of tears ran down her face. Her trembling hands cleaned her wet mouth. "Oh God, what I have done! I made my girl run away from me, from her sister." She screamed out for justice.

Chapter Eight

Alyona watched the multicolored lights glittering in the night through the falling snow. It was impossibly beautiful. She smiled. *It's all crazy... me and Bradley celebrating the New Year together.* "We can go to Austria and rent a nice chalet in the mountain," *he said.* Of course he had already thought of everything.

She didn't really have any big plans and a New Year holiday with a charming stranger in the Austrian mountains could be an unforgettable memory. Alyona knew very well what this holiday could mean. It was highly likely that she could fall for Bradley. She couldn't sleep. For long hours she found herself wondering what to do. She glanced at the clock. It was just after midnight. She felt like an idiot, thinking about the same thing continually. It was like she knew the answer, but at the same time she didn't really know. She had made many mistakes in her life, more than she could remember. However, since she met Bradley, she had felt joy without the need to pretend she was someone else. She pulled up the covers and closed her eyes, hopping the night would bring the right answer.

******

The phone rang and Alyona jumped off the bed. She feared the worst. She hoped nothing had happened to Bradley. The TV was flashing in the darkness, which was penetrating the whole room. Although it was almost morning, the thing that scared her most was the strange dream she had. The phone continued ringing on the bedside table. Alyona watched it, terrified. To answer? Or not to answer? In the end she decided to answer.

"Hello?"

She was still asleep, and she thought she heard a train.

"Hello?" She paused.

Yes, it was a train passing by. Alyona's became more terrified.

"Hello? Who's this?"

She heard some gasping and a voice burst out. "Alyona... Alyona..."

As she heard the voice on the other end of the line, Alyona felt her heart stop. It had been more than 13 years since she had heard that voice, but she could never forget it.

"Masha." She didn't know what to say.

"Alyona, our mother..." Masha paused for a while.

Was she crying? Alyona couldn't tell.

Masha's voice came back. "Alyona, you must come home..."

Alyona felt her heart pounding in her head. Now she was gasping for breath, too.

"Masha, what is it? Is everything alright?"

"Please come home. Our mother is not well, and she wants to see you..."

Alyona felt that the whole world was falling. She was half-asleep. Even though she was shaking and crying, she tried to sound strong. "Masha, I'll be there as soon as I can."

She didn't say anything else. She threw the receiver and went to the desk. She opened her computer and started searching for the first flight to Novosibirsk...

******

After his successful meeting in Brussels, Bradley couldn't wait to fly back to London. He couldn't wait to see Alyona. Even though it was late, he would visit her, just for a few minutes. He had to see her. He walked through the crowds to read the departure information on the screen. It was still early, so he stopped at the bar, set down his briefcase, and ordered an espresso. As he sat, he noticed a girl sitting across from him, staring at him insistently. Bradley tried to ignore her, but the girl began gesticulating, making faces to indicate that she wanted him to come over. Bradley glanced at her. Christ!

What did she want from him? She was without doubt a very sensual woman, but he wouldn't have more than one adventure with her if he didn't have anything better to do.

The girl stared at him, smiling quizzically. She probably knew what he was thinking. As he turned to the other side, he found the girl next to him.

"Hey, you. I noticed you're all alone. These business trips can be boring sometimes if you don't have company."

"Not for people like me," Bradley replied.

"We all need someone to keep us company, darling." The woman fished inside her oversize bag and produced a shiny black purse. She slipped out a card.

"Shouldn't the man ask for a number first?" Bradley said.

The girl shrugged. "Men are stupid these days. They don't have the guts for that."

Christ! This girl knew what she wanted, but she had chosen the wrong target. Bradley glanced at his watch. "If you'll excuse me, I have an airplane to catch." He picked up his briefcase and slipped away. Then he turned. "Save that card for someone else."

The girl watched him walk away. She didn't seem surprised. She found him a bit arrogant, but Bradley was sure she was used to that.

"British Airways flight to London Heathrow Airport is now boarding," announced a voice. *"Please have your boarding pass and identification ready for boarding. We would like to invite*

our first—and business-class passengers to board."

"Good afternoon, Sir. May I have your passport and ticket, please?"

"Here you go." Bradley gave the woman his passport.

"Thank you, Sir. I hope you have a nice flight back home." A sweet smile appeared on the woman's face as a background of full sunlight penetrated the airport window.

"Thanks."

A few minutes later, Bradley was settled in the airplane. He methodically sorted through his papers, placing them in tidy sections in his elegant leather briefcase.

"Chicken or pasta?"

"Sorry?" Bradley asked.

"Would you like chicken or pasta?"

"I'm fine, thank you."

"Anything to drink?"

"I'd have a glass of sparkling wine, please."

"Here you go."

"Thanks."

Bradley drank the wine with a sense of achievement. His business meeting had gone perfectly and now he was confident and full of dreams about the coming holiday with Alyona. Her words had touched his heart. He was happy to know that Alyona had the same feelings about him.

Chapter Nine

Picky started barking. He jumped around and went crazy at the door.

"What is it? What did you hear?" Alyona asked.

Another knock at the door increased Picky's frenzied response.

"Shhhh." Alyona walked slowly towards the door and looked through the peep hole. Bradley waved his hand. "It's me!"

"Just a minute!" Alyona looked in the mirror. She passed her hands through her hair, then pinched her cheeks a few times. When she finally opened the door, she realized she was wearing the citro top without anything underneath.

"Oh my gosh!" She ran back.

"Is that showing how happy you are to see me?" Bradley said as he placed his luggage in the hall.

"Make yourself comfortable. I'll be back in a minute."

"I sure will." He took off his coat and began browsing in the cozy house. The smell of cheese pie came from the kitchen. Picky curled up by the fireplace. The house wasn't big, but it was warm and comfortable.

Bradley picked up a book, curious to know what Alyona liked to read. As he sat on the comfortable sofa, sunk deep in the cushions, his eyes paused on a piece luggage next to the library furniture. He smiled with satisfaction, acknowledging that Alyona had made her decision to go with him to Austria. He breathed in deeply and tried to calm his emotion. He knew they would have fun together.

Alyona appeared from the other room. It had taken her a long time to find the right top.

"Finally." Bradley stood up and walked towards her.

"Sorry to make you wait." She tucked her hair behind her ear.

"That's alright. I like your top; matches your brown eyes." He leaned forward with wide arms and hugged her. "It's so good to see you. It seems like it's been forever."

"I'm happy to see you, too." She hurled herself into his arms. "You came just in time."

Bradley laughed and hugged her tightly. "In time for what?" he asked.

"I'll tell you later. Let's sit. How was your flight?"

"Long and boring," Bradley said.

"Hmm... you don't look bored. Rather happy."

"That's because I get to see you," he replied. Of course, he couldn't tell her about the incident with the girl in the airport.

"I'm going to get tea. Would you like some?"

"Tea?" he repeated. "I bought a quality red wine from the airport. We can have a glass of wine instead."

"Alright. I'll bring the glasses and some slices of cheese pie."

"I should wash my hands in the meantime," Bradley said.

"Sure, the bathroom is on the right-hand side, second door. The clean towels are folded next to the sink," she said.

In the meantime, Alyona went into the kitchen, took two glasses and a plate with the delicious cheese pie, and returned to the leaving room. She didn't want to say anything yet about her trip back home. Bradley seemed so happy to see her; how would he take the news when she told him she wasn't going with him to Austria?

"Come and sit down," he said as he opened the bottle of wine.

Alyona set down the glasses and the plate with pie and sat silently.

Bradley poured the wine and handed her a glass. "Is something wrong? Your mood changed suddenly."

"I'm good, better than I've ever been before."

Bradley extended his hand along the top of the sofa behind her head and looked at her intimately. "So, what have you been up to these two days?" he asked. "Of course, apart from thinking of me." He smiled teasingly.

She smiled, too. "I've been busy sorting things out. And if you're wondering whether I was thinking of you, yes, I was."

"That's a relief. For a moment I was concerned about that." Bradley drank his wine thoughtfully and watched her raise her glass to her lips—lips that he very much wanted to kiss. He cleared his throat. "I booked a cozy wooden chalet in Austria."

Alyona paused, holding the glass of wine in front of her mouth. "There's something I should tell you first."

"What is it?" Bradley asked, anxious to hear the answer.

"I'm not coming with you to Austria."

"You're not?" Bradley shook his head. "Have I done something wrong that made you change your mind?"

"Yes. I mean, no! You haven't done anything wrong. That's not why I changed my mind. My plans have changed."

"What do you mean by that? Have you met someone else?"

"No, of course not." She let out a smile.

"Then what is it? Can you just say it? I'm burning up here!"

"My mother isn't well; I need to go see her. I haven't seen her for a very long time, and now I feel guilty." She burst into tears.

"Hey, it's okay ... it's okay. I'll come with you." Bradley held her face in both hands, wiping her tears. He softly kissed her forehead.

Alyona took a few moments to consider his proposal. She couldn't even think about the idea of bringing a man home, not after all these years. "That's a good thought, but I need to do this on my own."

"How long are you going to be away?"

"I don't have the answer to that. I've been waiting for this to happen for so long." There was sadness and regret in her voice.

"I'm sorry. I had no idea you've been suffering so much. There's so much about you I don't know." His green eyes intensified. "I want to know everything about you, about your family. Tell me more. Tell me about your relationship with your mother. Why haven't you two seen each other for so long?"

Alyona looked at him and let out a small cry. "Maybe I'll tell you one day. It's so good having you here."

Bradley curled his arms around her body and in a soft voice, said, "It's good having you in my life."

Hearing these words, she slowly turned her head and met his gaze. They sat in silence for a moment—a very long moment. She finally said, "Maybe we should wait until I'm back. I don't want to complicate my situation now."

"I think getting to know you could simplify the situation. I want to take care of you and be there for you when you need me." Bradley ran his fingers over her face; it was warm, sweet, and innocent. "When are you leaving?"

"Tomorrow morning."

"Uh ... so soon." Bradley looked away. He was pale and sweaty.

"Are you alright?"

"I'm fine," he said. "I must be very tired after this wine."

"Why don't you stay here overnight? You can sleep on my bed, and I'll sleep on the couch."

Bradley wiggled his eyebrows. That was exactly what he wanted to hear. "And I can drop you at the airport tomorrow morning."

"Yes, you can," she whispered, pulling the end of his shirt collar so she could kiss his cheek. Kissing was fine; she felt herself blushing. Fortunately, Bradley wasn't as pale as he'd been before. She didn't know what he did, but it was a good trick. "Thank you," she added.

"For what?" Bradley swung his head around.

"For being so kind, and for being you..."

Before she could say anything else, Bradley covered her mouth with his fingers, then leaned forward. Their lips crushed together in a fiery, passionate and demanding kiss. Her heart fluttered inside her chest, and the whole word fell away. Their lips were moving in perfect sync. It was an intimate and electrifying kiss. For that single moment time stopped. It was just him and her. His fingers tangled in her long hair, pulling her into him. They paused, looking into each other's eyes. She swallowed and held her breath, then looked away for a moment. His eyes searched for hers, then drifted down to her lips. It felt good. It felt right. Alyona's lips curved into a smile and Bradley couldn't help but smile back. Alyona kissed his lips one more time, then slipped away from his arms. "I'll see you tomorrow morning."

This couldn't be happening again. Bradley couldn't believe it, but the look on her face told him everything. *I want you, but not tonight.* There was something unique about Alyona. She was different, she was beautiful, she was independent, she was cool, she was fun, she was everything...

* * * * * *

Everything was happening so fast. Too fast. It was like living in a dream. The best dream ever. The smell of fresh coffee woke up Bradley. He stretched his legs and bounded off the couch. Within a matter of seconds, he was in the kitchen.

"Good morning, sleepy!" Alyona said as Bradley walked into the kitchen.

"Good morning, juicy girl." He kissed her cheek. "I'm so hungry!"

"Breakfast is almost ready."

"Should I help?" Bradley asked, although he desperately needed a shower first.

"That's okay. You can make me breakfast next time." Alyona smiled.

"Sounds like a perfect deal." He smiled back. "I'll take a quick shower before you're finished."

"Alright, but don't be late."

"I'll be back before you know I'm gone." Bradley rushed off, took fresh clothes from his luggage and jumped into the shower.

Alyona continued preparing breakfast and waited for Bradley. She loved mornings. The cool breeze wafted in through the window. She gazed outside. The garden was very quiet. A fox walked through with its nose searching for food. Alyona had never liked foxes. She had no idea why, but she feared them. A few nights ago, she had been walking home when she heard a bump in the garden. Suddenly, a scrawny fox had come out. Alyona had screamed and run to her house as fast as she could. She had been shaking and in fear, her heart beating so hard it felt like it was going to pop out of her chest. She was terrified. Her body shivered again at the thought of that moment. She closed the window and returned to the kitchen.

"Okay, I'm ready." Bradley grabbed her hand and pulled her in for a quick kiss. "What was happening out there?"

"Um... no... nothing... I was just observing."

"I haven't seen Picky this morning," Bradley said.

"Oh... Nick, my friend, picked him up earlier. I asked him to look after Picky while I'm away."

"Ah. Why didn't you tell me? I'd have taken care of Picky."

"That's okay. I'm sure you have other things to do."

"Picky would be happier with me than with your friend."

Alyona smiled. "You still don't trust me?"

"Of course I do," Bradley said, then curled his arm around her waist.

"What time is your flight?" he asked as he placed his head over her shoulder.

"The flight takes off at 11:34 a.m. from Heathrow Airport."

Bradley glanced at his wrist; his clock indicated 6:30 a.m. "I think we should be alright."

"Yes, we should," Alyona replied.

"Promise you'll call me as soon you get there. And you won't forget about me."

"How could I forget you?" She gave him a mischievous smile as she got up and took their coffee cups to the kitchen. Bradley followed her with the other dishes.

"How long is the flight to your city?"

"Nine hours, if everything goes well. I'll need to stay in Moscow one night, and the next day take another flight to Novosibirsk."

"That's a long trip." He acknowledged.

"I'll be fine."

"I know you will. You're a strong woman, but you still need a man to take care of you."

"I may have found one." Alyona smiled and filled his heart with joy.

******

With breakfast over and the kitchen back in order, they were ready to leave. Bradley drove the car over to Alyona's house and helped with the luggage.

"Do you have everything?" he asked.

"Yes."

"Then we're ready to go." Bradley put on his seat belt and put the car in motion.

On their way to the airport, they were both silent. She didn't know what to say and he couldn't find the words to convince her to let him go with her.

"We're almost there," he finally said.

"I'll get my passport and ticket ready." She picked up her bag from the backseat while Bradley parked the car. "Oh my God! Oh my God! I can't find my ticket!" Alyona yelled in desperation.

"What do you mean you can't find it? Are you sure you brought it with you?"

"I'm 100 percent sure." Alyona began fishing out her stuff—books, makeup, creams, spray, magazines. "There's nothing here. Oh my God, I'm going to miss the flight."

"Check in your luggage," Bradley suggested.

"No, it can't be there. I know I had it here this morning." Alyona checked all the pockets of her bag.

Bradley removed her luggage from the car. "Are you sure you didn't put it inside one of these pockets?"

Alyona, jumped out of her seat, confused. "I might have put it there."

Bradley opened the zipper and fished out the ticket. "Is this what you're looking for?"

"Yes! Yes! That's the ticket. Oh, thank God." She hugged Bradley. "I need to run now. I'm late." She took her bag and walked away, then turned back. Bradley was still standing and watching her. "Sorry, I'm so stressed." She threw herself into his arms and kissed him.

Bradley had to admit that watching her leave was tough. He was scared he wouldn't see her again, scared of losing her. It had taken this to realize he was falling in love with her. He lowered his head. "I hope you have a safe trip, and please don't forget to call me."

"I'll call you." Alyona turned around one last time and waved goodbye with her right hand. She hoped she could return soon.

She hadn't meant to fall in love with Bradley, but it was happening. From the first time they met, she had known there was something special about him. He looked so sincere and true. Alyona had been hurt in the past and she didn't believe she would ever find the love of her life. Now she was living in that fantasy, that she had finally found her soul mate, her love, the man who would take care of her. She would never be lonely again.

******

Why was Bradley the one? She couldn't explain it, she just knew it was him. She felt the urge to scream out, *"I've finally found my real Love!"*

Chapter Ten

During the flight to Moscow, Alyona didn't feel well. She felt like throwing up, as she absolutely hated the smell of airplanes, but seeing her mother was worth all the suffering during the flight. After a few hours of sleep in the hotel airport, she was now settled in the airplane to Novosibirsk. "Fifteen minutes until we arrive at Tolmachevo Airport—Novosibirsk, our final destination," the flight attendant announced.

The plane slowly started to descend. It was 5:23 p.m. on January 2, 2001 and -17C when they landed. That was cold enough for Alyona; she wasn't used to the low temperatures anymore. The airport was just thirty 30 minutes by car from her mother's house. The air felt like ice. Alyona put on her hat, pulled her scarf tightly over her mouth and nose, and called for a taxi. A young man stopped the car next to her, and Alyona jumped inside. The driver settled her luggage, then sat behind the wheel, ready to go.

"It's freezing outside," Alyona said, holding her hands close to her mouth.

The young driver laughed, glancing at her in the rear-view mirror. She was obviously a beginner. He spent the whole day outside and in, with nothing more than a hat and coat. "You may need a few shots of vodka to keep you warm, Miss."

"I'll be fine as soon I get home," Alyona replied.

"There's a belief in Siberia that having a few shots of vodka will insulate you from the cold."

"I'll keep that in mind," she said.

The young driver smiled, displaying perfect teeth. He held her gaze and Alyona turned her head away, feeling embarrassed that he had noticed her looking at him. He was obviously a good-looking man, but nothing compared to Bradley. Alyona smiled with satisfaction. She glanced outside the window as the car stopped. A woman crossed the street, and Alyona watched her. She was dressed in a full-length fur coat, possibly white fox. That coat was likely warm and more comfortable than one would expect.

A few minutes later, the car stopped again and Alyona was surprised to see her childhood home. It hadn't changed much. Nothing had changed, actually.

"Here we go, Miss."

"Thank you!" After giving the driver a good tip, Alyona got out of the car. She felt a bit dizzy. Was that because of the different time zone? Or were these the emotions of seeing her mother again? She took a deep breath. The air was even colder, but she needed to refresh herself.

******

The door of the little room opened and Serafima burst into tears as Alyona entered. "Mother…." Alyona made her way towards her mother's bed and hugged her for the first time in 13 long years. It was a hug they couldn't hold tightly enough.

"I love you! I love you!" said her mother.

For the first time in 13 years, Alyona felt that she belonged. She felt like she was floating. It was surreal.

"My little girl. I missed you so much." Serafima couldn't stop the tears from running down her cheeks. "Please don't hate me for what I said. I never wanted you to leave this house. I understood my errors too late."

"Mother, I don't hate you. I can't tell you how much I've missed you all these years." Returning home was like removing a heavy stone from Alyona's heart.

"Forgive me for letting you down when you needed me most. I was punishing you for things you had never done."

"That's all right, Mother. I forgot about that a long time ago." Alyona caressed her mother's old face, wiping her tears with her hand. She noticed her mother had lost some weight since she had last seen her. "I love you, I always did." Alyona kissed her mother's hands.

"Oh, my dear, you have such a good soul and heart. I don't deserve your love," said her mother.

"Don't say that, Mother. Nothing can change my love for you. I'm so happy I'm finally home." Alyona's eyes filled with tears. This was a moment Alyona hadn't thought possible. The reunion was extremely emotional, and not just for Alyona and her mother. Masha was standing by the door in silence.

Alyona watched her sister wordlessly. Masha's blonde hair was shorter than it used to be. Her eyes seemed smaller, and her body looked weak. Masha had changed a lot; she was 38 years old. Alyona wondered if Masha had a boyfriend or husband. For a moment, Alyona felt good about herself—for being fit, for dressing better, for having a career. She wanted so badly to show her sister that she'd made it. It would be nice if, for once, Masha could say, "You're good, and I was wrong about you." Her jealousy had destroyed their family and forced Alyona to leave.

Serafima took a long look at her two daughters, who were now two women.

"I know you two have never been on the best of terms, but I think it's time to forget that," Serafima said.

Alyona wasn't usually lost for words, but she didn't know what to say.

Her mother spoke in an admonishing tone. "One day I might not be here, but I want you two to be a family as we used to be. I want you two to love each other."

"Mother, what are you talking about? You'll be here with us for many years to come," Alyona said.

Serafima glanced at Alyona. She felt seized by a mixture of guilt and regret. She shouldn't have let this happen between her daughters. "You are both my own blood, and I dearly wish that you two would put the past aside and move on."

Any reminder of the past pained Alyona; she didn't want to think about it any longer. She had made mistakes, too. Running way had been an easy way to escape her problems. She should have tried a reconciliation. Instead, she had chosen the easy way while Masha had looked after their mother.

"How are you, Masha?" Alyona tried to put on a good face, forcing a smile.

"I'm doing well," Masha replied. "I want to say how sorry I am for being so stupid. I was jealous of you. You were beautiful and smart, and I couldn't cope with that. But since you left, I realized how wrong I was. Everything in my life was empty without you. Our lives have never been the same. Mother got ill and she never smiled." Tears fell from Masha's eyes, down her skinny face to her mouth and under her chin.

Alyona stood up and walked towards her sister. "Please don't cry. We were two silly little girls, and I wasn't an angel, either."

They gazed at each other for long seconds. Then they both burst into laughter as they realized how stupid they had been. Alyona cried too, but they were tears of happiness. They kissed and hugged each other like two friends who hadn't seen each other in a while.

"I want to hear all about you and your life in London. I heard it's very beautiful. I'd like to go there one day," Masha whispered.

"And you will, but now I'm curious to know about you and your life here in Novosibirsk. Do you have a boyfriend? Are you seeing someone?" Alyona asked.

Watching the two sisters chatting and laughing, Serafima couldn't stay in her skin. *"God, thank you for listening to my prayers."*

"I'm seeing someone," Masha whispered. "I was thinking, now that you're here, you may want to keep Mother company so I can go out sometimes."

"Of course I will. We'll talk about this tomorrow. Let's go back to Mother."

✳✳✳✳✳✳

The three women sat and had a long chat. After hours, late in the night, Alyona finally settled in her room. She started unpacking, then rested. When she woke up, it was late morning. Masha got the tea ready and the daughters sat together with their mother, drinking the tea and conversing about what had changed in Novosibirsk, who had gotten married, who was still single... they gossiped for hours.

Later, Alyona and Masha went for a walk. Masha showed Alyona what was new in the city. They got sushi, and they talked and laughed at all the differences and similarities between Novosibirsk and London. The nostalgia of Novosibirsk softened Alyona's heart. The Siberian city was beautiful, just as she remembered. She didn't even feel the cold winter she had noticed when she got off the plane. Of course, this time she was dressed warmly, even though it was uncomfortable and unfashionable. She didn't care much. The only problem about Siberia was the wardrobe—too hot in the summer and too cold in the winter. These were really the only two seasons of note in Novosibirsk, since both spring and autumn arrived and departed so quickly, they were hardly noticeable.

After a couple of hours, the sisters stopped to drink Russian vodka at the local bar. Alyona felt that she was in a different world. The snow-flakes started to fall, and she began singing like a little kid. The romance of the place was infectious. They passed the opera house, which announced that the Christmas concert would be a success. According to the old Julian calendar, Novosibirsk celebrated the Orthodox Christmas on the 7th of January, which meant that Alyona would finally celebrate her own Christmas with her mother and sister. She smiled. *It's so funny to realize how easy it is to slip from one reality to another.*

Chapter Eleven

With Alyona back home, Serafima, her mother, began feeling better—every single day like a new beginning. Alyona learned how to cook her mother's recipes. She prepared an abundant amount of fresh food every meal. Serafima couldn't remember the last time she had eaten so many different types of food.

"Mother, do you mind if I steal Masha for a few hours?"

"No. Steal away," said Serafima.

"Aren't you curious where we're going?"

"Nah, you two need to spend lots of time together after all these years apart. But, now that you ask, you've made me want to know where you two are going."

Alyona laughed.

"There's just three days left before our Orthodox Christmas and I realized we don't have a Christmas tree. I want to take Masha with me to help me choose one."

"Christmas tree?" Masha said. "We stopped doing that a long time ago."

"It's time to bring back that tradition," said Serafima. She was happy that Alyona wanted to do it. She hadn't seen a Christmas tree in her house for a long time.

"First, I have to finish dusting and cleaning. Then we can go," Masha said.

"Oh girl, you and your obsession about cleaning. Go and help your sister buy the Christmas tree."

"Let's go, Masha. I'll help you with the cleaning when we're back," Alyona suggested.

* * * * * *

Snow fell from the Siberian sky, covering the sidewalks and trees. The wind blew so hard, Alyona had trouble walking. It was the kind of freezing wind that bit at one's skin. By the time they got to the market, her cheeks were red and her nose was running from the cold.

"Let's stop at this little coffee shop and warm ourselves before we buy the Christmas tree," Masha suggested.

Alyona nodded, holding her scarf over her mouth.

Masha went first and Alyona followed her. Inside, it was warm and dry. A fire burned in the old stone fireplace. They ordered hot chocolate and sat at the table, warming their hands on the mugs, listening to the fire crackling.

Masha smiled as she looked at Alyona. For the first time, she felt so connected to her sister. She felt closer than she ever had before.

* * * * * *

After enduring the cold and a few falls into the snow, Alyona and Masha finally managed to bring home a Christmas tree. Alyona breathed in the natural fragrance. This Christmas tree had a completely different smell from the one she had in London. It smelled of oranges. She put on the candles, realizing they were the same decorations she had used 13 years ago. They hadn't been used much since then.

"Masha, can you pass me the gold decorations from the other box?"

"Where is it?"

"Behind you, right there, next to the box with the lights. Got it?"

"Yes, here you go." Masha stretched and handed her the box.

Everything was peaceful and quiet. Alyona began singing "Jingle Bells" and Masha joined in. Then they both stopped. They knew the joy of celebrating would be different if their mother could walk. They looked at each other with unspoken words; sorrow filled their faces. Then Alyona came up with a great idea. "We're two strong women; both of us can bring

Mother here so she can watch when we turn on the lights."

"Yes, let's do that," Masha agreed.

"I'm sure you two need some help over there?" said a voice from the other side of the room.

Masha's eyes grew wide as she turned towards the door. Alyona lifted her head; the decorative globes in her hand fell to the floor and broke into small pieces. "Mother! Mother!" Alyona yelled as loud as she could. She ran at the door and threw herself into her mother's arms. She began crying, but this time the tears were ones of happiness. "Mother! Are you walking?".

"I was feeling bored and lonely inside that room. I tried to put my feet on the floor, and I felt a hand touch them. I stood up and began to walk."

"Jesus, this is a miracle!" said Alyona.

"Masha, come here," Serafima called.

Masha was still in shock. She couldn't believe her eyes. She set down the box and walked towards the door.

Serafima held her two daughters in her arms and raised her head. *"Thank you! Thank you for making this miracle possible."*

They laughed and cried at the same time. Serafima had been set free from the constant pain she had suffered for years. God had given Serafima and her two daughters the greatest gift she could ever receive.

* * * * * *

After dinner, Serafima and her two daughters sat by the fireplace. She told them the story of how she had met their father, who, sadly, had died during an expedition in the Siberian mountains. A windstorm had killed him in the middle of nowhere. His body had been found covered with snow about a mile from his tent. This had happened exactly one week before his and Serafima's ten-year wedding anniversary. Serafima told her daughters how much she had loved her husband, but unfortunately, she hadn't had enough time to show him. When they first met, they fell madly in love. Their hidden love story continued for years. Then Serafima became pregnant. Alexei gathered all his courage and went to her house to ask her parents for permission to marry their daughter. Less than one month later, they were married. During her fifth month of pregnancy, Serafima had a miscarriage. "It was a boy," Serafima said.

"Alexei went into a depression, he wanted that boy so much. It took me long years, but then I got pregnant with Masha. Then, after another long gap, I got pregnant with you." Serafima reached for Alyona's hand. "Your father and I were so in love. We were the perfect couple. Alexei may not be here to see you, but I know he's looking at us right now." Serafima kissed Alyona's head. "You look so much like him."

Alyona smiled. "What a beautiful story," she said. She thought about Bradley. The last time they spoke was when she had called him from Moscow. However, something had gone wrong. When Bradley picked up the phone, and as Alyona had opened her mouth to say "hi," she heard him whispering at someone to be quiet. Alyona had held her breath.

"Hey, is everything okay?" Bradley said after a long moment.

Is he trying to play with me? Or is he really so stupid as to think I didn't hear another woman's voice?

"Yep, everything's great. I'm at the Moscow airport—at the hotel right now. Flying to Novosibirsk tomorrow." *Why am I explaining this to him? He doesn't care what I'm doing anyway. He seems very busy at the moment.*

"So, happy to go home?" Back in London, Bradley looked at the girl; his hand was raised to her mouth, as he was trying to shut her up.

"Yep, very happy," Alyona said.

"Do you know what time you're gonna get there tomorrow?"

"Nope, not sure." *Why do I have to tell him? It's none of his business.*

They stood quietly for a few seconds. Alyona felt uncomfortable. Bradley broke the ice. "Well, I have to go now. Call me once you get home."

"Yeah. Goodbye, Bradley." Alyona hung up the phone. She had the weirdest feeling in her stomach.

"Bye..." Bradley hated himself for what he had done. He took out his black leather wallet, wrote a £10.000 cheque and put it into the girl's hand. He closed her fist. "This is the last time you'll see money from me. Make sure you don't come back; otherwise I'll be forced to call the police."

"Ugh..." The girl rolled her eyes and shook her head. "You can't do that."

"Watch me!" Bradley said.

"You really love that girl, don't you?"

"Yes, I do, and I won't allow anyone to ruin our relationship. So don't waste your time around here."

"Ugh, I've never seen you like this. Anyway, I have a boyfriend now. I don't need you."

"Good. Make sure you don't need my money, too."

"I need this money to cover an old debt. I don't want to let know my new boyfriend that I'm broke."

Bradley opened the door, gesticulating with his head for her to leave.

"Okay, okay. I get it. I'm going..."

"Goodbye, Jessica."

Jessica stared at him for several moments. Sadly, she realized that she had lost Bradley forever.

Chapter Twelve

The previous night, there had been a lot of snow. Now Alyona and Masha were out in the yard making a snow mountain. When a snowball hit Alyona's hat, Alyona raised her head and saw her mother on the balcony, making a snowball. Serafima then threw the snowball at Masha and smiled. Alyona smiled back. That meant only one thing – a snowball fight between her and Masha! Part of Alyona told her that she was too old for this, but the freshly fallen snow was irresistible. As she turned, she saw Masha behind her, plunging her gloved hands into the snow and frantically making a stockpile of snowballs with which to retaliate.

"You're gonna lose, Masha!" Alyona said.

"Yeah, wanna bet?" Masha began throwing the snowballs.

Alyona throw another one and hit her. Masha was such a lousy shot, if she had 10 snowballs she would hit Alyona with maybe one. A nagging voice in Alyona's head told her to let Masha win, but she just couldn't. A snowball fight was a war and wars just had to be won.

"C'mon, Masha!" Serafima shouted from the balcony.

Another voice from the street shouted loudly, encouraging the fight. *"Go girls!"*

As Alyona looked over the garden, a snowball flew out of Masha's hand, hitting Alyona in the face. *Fights aren't meant to be fair, they're meant to be won.*

However, it was too early for Masha to sing victory.

Alyona's woolen gloves picked up the snow like they wanted to be snowballs themselves. The snow crystals began to freeze her fingers to the point that they no longer wanted to bend. However, cold or not, Alyona didn't want to give up.

After a while, Masha stopped. Her hands were frozen, too, and her lips tinged blue.

Alyona looked down at her feet; she had at least 20 snowballs, but Masha couldn't bend to grab one. Alyona dropped her own snowballs. A win would be sweet, but seeing her sister wet, her body almost immobile, Alyona decided to end the fight.

"Let's get inside, Masha," Alyona suggested. However, as she turned away, a snowball hit the back of her neck. Masha still hadn't had enough. Alyona had no choice. After a few minutes of intense fighting, Masha couldn't take any more; Alyona took home the snowball fight victory.

"You owned me," Masha said.

"I've never had so much fun in my life." Alyona smiled.

Masha stepped forward and the sisters gave each other a high-five.

"Let's get inside. I'm freezing. I can't feel my fingers and the snow on my clothes is frosting up," Masha said.

"I'm feeling cold, too. I need to change my clothes and then run into the city. I still need to buy a few things for tomorrow," Alyona said.

"Do you want me to come with you?" Masha asked.

"Oh, no, no, that's okay. I can do this on my own. You stay with our mother; she may need you."

The days had gone by very quickly and Alyona still hadn't had a chance to buy Christmas gifts for her sister and mother. Masha had been with her all the time. Alyona hopped to find something special for them today.

* * * * * *

"Alyona! Is that you?"

Alyona was standing by the till; waiting for the girl to wrap the cashmere sweater she had just bought for her mother, when she heard a voice behind her. She looked up and saw a man standing a few steps behind her. She slowly turned her head back to the cashier. *Who is that men? And how does he know my name?* It was the first good-looking man she had seen since she returned to Novosibirsk. She turned her head to look at him one more time. He smiled sweetly. She couldn't wrap her mind around the thought that he knew her, but as soon he smiled, something told her she had seen that grin before. He was tall, with light brown hair and smooth, perfect skin. His cheeks and nose were slightly red from the cold air. He was damn good looking. He looked much younger than she was; he couldn't have been one of her schoolmates. Alyona was curious to find out how he knew her. She took her bags with the gifts and, before leaving the shop, turned and smiled at the man. He walked outside after her.

"I can see you got used to our weather very quickly," he said.

"It's damn cold, but I'm still enjoying it," Alyona said, moving her bags from one hand to the other. "I'm sorry. Have we met before?"

"Oh, don't apologize. I'm sure you meet many people. Must be difficult to remember all their faces."

Alyona smiled. She hadn't met one person in the past week.

"Am I so funny that I make you smile?"

"No, no, you go ahead."

"Well, maybe you don't remember me, but you're beautiful enough for me to remember you."

Alyona laughed. *Damn it! Is he going to tell me where we met?*

"I'm Ivan. I dropped you off from the airport last week. You were completely frozen and I suggested that you take a shot of vodka."

Alyona blinked a few times, as she couldn't believe how different he looked outside that old car. "Sorry. What are you doing here?"

"Well, I live here," Ivan said.

"Oh, that makes sense." She smiled.

Ivan smiled back. He couldn't take his eyes off her. They passed the corner shop and crossed the busy road – the same road where Alyona and her sister had vodka a few days before.

"Look!" Ivan gestured. "There's a great bar. They serve the best vodka. I propose we go inside and have some shots. It's too cold to walk outside."

"I can't. I'm already late. My mother is waiting for me."

"Just one drink. I promise. Then I'll drop you off at home. Please don't invent any excuses."

"Okay, but I'll have a hot drink instead of vodka."

"I'm fine with that. Let's get inside," Ivan said. He took her bags, then grabbed her hand and pulled her inside the exclusive bar. Just like that. He didn't even ask her permission. Alyona opened her mouth to say something, but then she realized she didn't mind him holding her frozen hand. She felt the comfort of his warm hand over hers, and she felt good.

Ivan set down the bags, then helped her take off her coat and the big scarf wrapped around her neck. As she turned to sit, Ivan glanced at her body. His eyes traveled from her legs to her beautiful shoulders. *She's so perfect!*

Alyona rolled her eyes, as she could read his mind. She looked at him with her astonishingly beautiful eyes and Ivan felt embarrassed by his own thoughts.

"So, what would you like to drink?" he asked.

"I'll go for tea vprikusku."

"Okay, great, but I'm allowed to have one vodka?" He smiled.

"Yes, you are." She smiled back.

"Can I ask you something?"

"Yes, you can."

"Do you have a boyfriend?"

Alyona looked at him for a long few seconds. She didn't know how to answer.

"Well, it's a bit complicated, but yes, I'm seeing someone."

"What kind of complication? If I may ask. Your boyfriend turned out to be a not-very-nice man? He's living a secret life? He's been lying to you?"

"What? Why would you say that?"

"Well, because all men are the same."

"Right. And you're saying you're not part of that category?"

"Let's say I'm old-fashioned. I respect women. Maybe this is what makes me special."

Alyona wasn't sure why Ivan had asked her if she had a boyfriend and what he meant about a secret life, but she wanted to prove him wrong.

"You're right, people shouldn't tell lies, and I'm happy I can trust my boyfriend."

Ivan glanced at her. "You don't need to mention how much you trust your boyfriend. That would be a bad lie... wouldn't it?"

"What? Where did this come from?"

"I can see it; you have that kind of look in your eyes."

"Seriously! What kind of look do I have?"

"Like you're cross at him. Am I right?"

Alyona glanced at her watch. "It's getting late; I have to go now."

"That's an elegant way to avoid the answer."

Alyona laughed. It was the first time someone had laughed at him in that ironic way, but for some reason, Ivan liked it. "I'll drive you home," he said.

"Okay, then, let's go."

They got into the car, and after a few right and left turns, they reached her mother's house.

"Thank you for the lift," she said.

"Thank you for having a drink with me," Ivan replied.

"My pleasure."

Ivan smiled into the darkness. Her answer gave him the courage say, "We'll have to do this again."

"Oh, I don't think I'll have the time. I want to stay with my mother as much as I can. I haven't seen her in a very long time."

Ivan stared at her; he couldn't accept "no" for an answer. "Whenever you need a taxi, you know who to call." He gave her shoulder a small squeeze. "I'll never charge you. Wherever you want to go, I'll drop you off."

Alyona smiled. "You have something special, don't you?"

"I hope so."

"You aren't sure?"

"I'm very sure, but with you I'm scared of losing it."

"Don't say that. You won't."

Ivan watched Alyona walk away, waving her feminine hand in the air. She was a very smart woman, but this didn't put him off. He could see that she hadn't been happy to speak about her boyfriend. *I'll make sure she forgets about him soon. I'll take her mind off him. One day she'll thank me for that...*

Chapter Thirteen

January 6, 2001—day before Orthodox Christmas in Russia

A snowstorm had transformed the town of Novosibirsk into a romantic heaven. The temperature had dropped to -24C. However, this morning the sun rose bright and beautiful. The Siberian city was ready to celebrate the Orthodox Christmas. The house was full of joy and happiness, not just because of the holiday season, but because Serafima and her two daughters were together as a family.

After spending all day in the kitchen, Alyona anxiously wondered when they were going to eat. Cooking the Christmas Eve dinner with her mother, it had been hard to resist the food, but she had to. Her mother always had an eye on her. By tradition, on the Orthodox Christmas Eve, eating was forbidden before the first star appeared in the sky. Christmas was the end of 40 days of fasting, and Serafima still respected that tradition.

They all sat in the living room, waiting for the first star to appear. The twinkling lights of the Christmas tree illuminated the room with different colors. Christmas songs played. Alyona and Masha sat on the sofa, preparing their playing cards. Alyona glanced at her mother, sitting by the fireplace on her favorite wooden rocking chair. An old Christmas song came on the radio. They listened for a few seconds, then looked at each other. They were so happy together. However, listening to the song brought a mixture of feelings of sadness and regret. The acknowledgment that they had wasted so many years apart brought tears to their eyes.

"Mother, would you join us for a round of cards?" Alyona broke the tension of the moment.

"No, you two carry on. I'm feeling good here warming my feet by the fire," Serafima said as she gripped her hands on the chair and pushed back her head. She felt relaxed. Her body moved back and forth in the wooden rocking chair. Her gaze moved slowly from Alyona to Masha. She watched them playing cards and giggling on the sofa. It was such a beautiful moment. Observing her two daughters together warmed her heart.

"You girls should get ready to look for the new star tonight," said Serafima.

"What is all this fuss about the new star?" Alyona asked.

"When you see the new star, it means Jesus is born. Have you forgotten your own religion?" said her mother.

"No, Mother, of course not," Alyona replied. She was confused. Celebrating Christmas in London for so many years had become a habit. For a second, she hadn't remembered that according to the Orthodox Christmas in Russia, following the Julian calendar, Jesus had been born on the 7th of January. The irony was that if she was now in London, she would have remembered as she had done in the years past.

******

Alyona stretched her spine, tilting her head from side to side. She ran her hands through her long, dark hair and got up from the sofa to stand by the window. She watched the colorful lights playing over the white snow. The garden was quiet, very quiet. It was so different from London, and she enjoyed every moment of it.

"Alyona, come over here. The movie is about to start," Masha called.

"I'm coming," Alyona replied. She loved Christmas movies; she always had. She would stay there all night long, watching and dreaming at a perfect love story. She was hopelessly romantic when it came to the holiday season. She sighed deeply and threw herself into the sofa. Her baggy t-shirt slipped down to her shoulder, showing her beautiful smooth skin. She felt good and allowed herself the simple pleasure of being home. Although she wasn't wearing makeup and, after dinner, had swapped her beautiful mint green dress for more comfortable clothing, she still looked exceptionally pretty.

Next to her, Masha laughed loudly. Masha always laughed at every single movie scene. She had such a comical laugh, but sometimes it got annoying.

Alyona smiled brightly. Tonight she felt good. Masha's laugh didn't bother her.

"Are you having fun, Masha?"

"Yeah, this movie is freaking awesome."

"I know. I've seen this movie at least five times, but I still enjoy it."

It was one of those movies that plays every Christmas Eve, but Alyona still couldn't get enough of it because the adrenaline pumped through her during every scene. The movie was always so much fun.

******

Just after midnight, a car pulled up next to Alyona's mother's home. The house stood out from the others, as it was lit up with cheer. A beautiful tree in the front window contained bright, colorful lights. The house was old, but well maintained. A Santa sleigh and reindeer had been placed on the roof. The snow swirled, making the holiday scene complete. It was like the setting of a magical Christmas tale. There was no denying that the home had the feel of the spirit of Christmas.

The doorbell rang and Masha rolled her eyes. "Mother, how many Carol singers we've received today!"

"I think these are the last ones. Go and give them some money," said her mother.

"We've had enough singers tonight. Let them go." Masha turned back to watch the movie.

The doorbell continued to ring insistently.

"Go and give them some money, Masha! This people don't leave easily," said her mother.

"I think I've already given all my money to Carol singers," Masha replied.

"I have some change in my bag," Alyona said, stretching her legs on the sofa.

Masha got up. Moving her body lazily, she took some money from Alyona's purse and went to the door. *I'm gonna get rid of these people.* She opened the door and extended her hand with the coins. The person outside the door stared at the money and then stepped back to get a better view of Masha. He watched her with curiosity.

"What are you looking at? We gave less money to the others singers," Masha said.

The man smiled, and Masha's expression changed. "You're not one of the Carol singers, are you?" Masha looked at him more closely. "Of course, look at you. Your coat is too expensive for this job!"

The man stood in silence. He watched Masha, amused. "No, I'm not a Carol singer," he finally answered. "But I sing songs sometimes...."

"So, who are you, then?" Masha asked.

"I'm a friend of Alyona's. Is she home?"

"Alyona doesn't have many friends in town. Do you have a name?"

"I certainly do."

"Who's there, Masha?" her mother called out. "Give them the money and come inside. It's freezing out there."

After another few minutes, the door closed and Masha came inside. "Alyona, someone is asking about you," Masha said as she walked back into the living room.

"And who might that be?" Alyona asked, without bothering to turn around. She was concentrating on the end of movie, which had brought her to tears.

"You can see yourself!" Masha said, slightly raising the tone of her voice.

Alyona turned her head. Her eyes changed expression as she saw the man beside Masha. She stood, speechless for long seconds. This was the last thing she had expected. She stared at the man, dumb. Masha and her mother looked at each other, confused.

"Bradley! What are you doing here?" Alyona finally spoke.

"I came to see you."

"How did you find me?"

Bradley pulled out a book. "You dropped this in my car..."

"That's my book," Alyona said.

"I know. I found out it's yours when the letter inside it fell out. I read your mother's address on it, so I decided to come over and return it."

"I was desperately looking for this book. I thought I had left it on the airplane." Alyona grabbed the book and began flipping through the pages.

Serafima watched Alyona, impatient. "Well, now that you found your book, are you going to introduce this young man to us?" she said.

"Oh, sorry. This is my mother Serafima, and this is my sister Masha.

Mother and Masha, this is Bradley."

Bradley stepped forward. "I'm very pleased to meet you both." He shook Serafima's hand and hugged her cordially. He did the same with Masha.

"It's so nice to have such a man in our house on Christmas Eve, isn't it, Alyona?" Serafima said.

"Um... yeah... it's good..." Alyona still couldn't believe that Bradley had flown to Siberia for her.

Bradley smiled as he noticed her disbelief. He stepped back, then leaned in and kissed her cheek. "You look gorgeous."

"So do you." Alyona blushed.

Bradley curled his arms around her waist and hugged her. "I missed you," he whispered into her ear.

Alyona didn't reply to that, but he knew she missed him too. He could tell.

"So Bradley, tell me more about yourself. How did you meet my daughter?" Serafima asked.

"We're neighbors and we share the same garden." He smiled as he glanced at Alyona, rubbing her fingers.

"Your relationship with my daughter must be more than neighbors, as you flew here to see her. I don't think you came all this way just to return a book," Serafima insisted. "Mother, Bradley and I, we're just..."

"Let me say this." Bradley interrupted her. "I'm Alyona's fiancé. We're engaged." He grabbed Alyona's hand, kissed it and pressed it to his chest.

Serafima smiled. "Alyona, why didn't you tell us anything about this handsome man?"

"Well, I... um..." *I didn't know I was engaged until now.*

"I think she wanted to wait until you got better," Bradley said.

"Yes, that's right. Seeing you lying in that bad... it wasn't a good time for this news."

"Well, now I'm perfectly fine and I'm ready for this news. Welcome to our family, Bradley." Serafima opened her arms to him.

This can't be true. Alyona found it hard to believe how things had turned out. What would her mother say when she found out this was just a lie? Why had Bradley come out with this fake affirmation?

"Alyona, why don't you show Bradley your room so he can settle in and get comfortable?"

"Oh, Mother, we can give him the guest room. It's more spacious."

"The guest room? Why would you put your fiancé in the guest room? I'm sure it's not the first time you two have shared a room," Serafima said.

Alyona shook her head. *Damn Bradley.*

The whole situation amused Bradley and he let out a laugh. He expected Alyona to laugh too, but she didn't. He looked at her. There was no sign of a smile on her face.

Away from the others, Alyona gave him a sharp look. "I know what you're thinking, but this isn't a joke, and since you don't know my mother, you are to exchange no more than a few words with her. You don't have the right to hurt her."

"True, but for the little we've spoken, I get the feeling she likes me."

"That's not enough. You can't come out with that lie."

"But, I was serious. I wasn't lying."

"Oh, please. Can you stop pretending you were serious?"

"I'm serious. You don't look happy to see me."

"My room is over there," she indicated.

"That's really not answering my question, is it?"

"Bradley, I called you, and you were with another woman just one day after I left London. What do you want from me now?" There was sadness in her voice. A few tears dripped from her eyes and fell over her cheeks. She turned her head and with a fast movement wiped way the tears, hoping Bradley hadn't noticed.

Bradley placed his hand on her shoulder. "I'm so sorry. I didn't want to hurt you."

His touch made her look up. "That's okay. It's my fault. I shouldn't have followed my instincts so blindly."

"Please don't say that. That woman you heard over the phone was my ex-girlfriend. It's been finished between us for a long time. She came to ask for money. I don't even know how she found out where I live. I'm so sorry about this misunderstanding and I promise you will never see or hear about her again."

"I can't believe you, Bradley."

"You honestly think I came here to return your book? I came here because I knew you were upset with me and I wanted to clarify."

"Sorry, but you were whispering at her to be quiet. Why would you do that if you had nothing to hide?"

"Because I didn't know what to do and I didn't want you to hear a woman's voice on my phone. I'm not good at these things. But I'm with you right now, and I can't hold back this burning desire to kiss you."

Alyona looked away. Bradley pulled her over to him and wrapped his arms around her. He raised her chin with his fingers and smiled at her. Alyona breathed deeply. She drew him towards her with her eyes; her face was blushing. She was incredibly gorgeous. Bradley held her close, gently running his fingers through her silky hair, inhaling the fresh scent of her shampoo. With both his hands, he grabbed her right hand and placed her open palm on his heart, holding it there. He stared at her, his eyes exuding love and protection. Her heart beat faster as his face approached hers. He kissed her softly at first, then began to bite gently at her lips, sending wild tremors along her spine. It was a sensation she had never known she was capable of feeling, and it made her want even more.

Bradley stopped and looked into her eyes once again. Then his mouth covered hers with a hungry kiss. Alyona opened her mouth with a moan and before she knew it, she was kissing him back. She fell into a dizzy, swaying world.

Suddenly, Alyona pushed away, moving her hands in the air. "I'm sorry, Bradley, but I don't think this right."

"What... what do you mean?"

"Why did you tell my mother we're engaged?"

"Because that's what I want." He said.

"Bradley, we don't even know each other very well. We've met only a few times..."

"True. I don't know much about you, but I'm learning fast, and all I know is that you're the woman I want to wake up next to in the morning." Bradley held her head with both his hands and rested his forehead against hers. He kissed her lips softly. "I need you in my life," he said.

Alyona stared at him. *If he just knew that I need him more than he needs me.*

******

It was late morning when Alyona woke up. She looked around. Bradley wasn't in bed. She looked at his opened luggage. Ah, he should be around somewhere. She gazed outside the window. *"Oh my God, it's Christmas!"* She got dressed and went to her sister's room to wake her up."It's Christmas!" Alyona shouted as she opened the door. She saw that Masha wasn't there, either. She heard Christmas music coming from downstairs, so Alyona made her way to the living room.

The TV was on and Masha was adding small pieces of wood to the fireplace. Bradley was vividly engaged in a conversation with her mother. He gestured with his hands and her mother started laughing.

Alyona walked down the stairs and they all went silent.

"Oh, here you're, sleepyhead," Serafima said.

"Good morning, Mother. Why didn't anybody wake me up?"

"That's okay, Masha and I got the table ready for lunch. And Bradley was a big help getting the wood ready for the fireplace."

"Oh, really! I didn't know you're good at that."

"You don't know many other good things about me."

"Well, I hope to have the opportunity to find out one day." Alyona said.

"I'll make sure you do." Bradley smiled.

Serafima smiled, too. "Would you like a cup of tea, darling?"

"No, I'm okay, Mother." Alyona gazed at Bradley sitting on the sofa. She didn't remember for how long she had been lost in the darkness the previous night, or what exactly had taken place. The lights were off in her room, though the lights from the decorations outside had danced across her body. The white sheets were wrapped around her hands. Bradley's soft lips had kissed her body. And then she saw Bradley on the top of her. They were having sex. She couldn't remember anything else. How had she gotten to that point?

Hold on. I remember Bradley opening a bottle of a liquor. I had a few small glasses, but that wouldn't get me drunk. This can't be right. I had sex with Bradley, and I don't even remember it very well. But I know I enjoyed it. She gave him a look when he wasn't watching. *Maybe he doesn't remember it, either. How should I ask him: "Did we really have sex last night? Because I'm not very sure?" He's gonna think I'm an alcoholic. No, better not say anything. Let him speak first.*

She raised her head and saw Bradley watching her.

For God's sake, why is he staring at me?

"Hi. Did you sleep well?" he asked.

Alyona raised her head. The way she looked at him knocked him out. He was cooked for her.

"Hi... um... yes, yes I did," she replied, playing with her hair.

Bradley smiled, and she blushed. She felt butterflies in her stomach. She didn't know if it was the liquor that had made her feel dizzy last night or Bradley, with his sensual way of looking at her. She lowered her head, as she wasn't prepared to face his gaze. She remembered last night, screaming his name. His passion had rolled over her, and she had forgotten that she should be upset with him.

"Well, now that we're all here, let's open these presents. Shall we?" Serafima said.

"Yes, let's start with yours, Mother," Alyona suggested.

"Yeah, open yours, Mother," Masha said from beside her.

Serafima grabbed a red box and began slowly unwrapping the paper. After she opened the box, she pulled out a beautiful scarf.

Alyona looked at her sister. *Where did Masha buy that scarf?*

Masha looked at Alyona and shrugged her shoulders. *Where did that expensive scarf come from?*

Serafima got up and hugged Bradley. "Thank you! This is so beautiful!"

"No, thank you for your warm hospitality," Bradley said.

Alyona and Masha smiled at each other. Then they began opening the gifts, one at a time. Bradley took lots of pictures all the while.

Now there was just one gift left, and nobody picked it up.

"I think that's your gift, Alyona," said her mother.

"No, Mother, I opened mine already."

"Your name's written on it." Masha went over to read it out loud.

"Oh, Mother. You shouldn't. I'm happy with the gifts you've already given me."

"C'mon, what are you waiting for? Open it!" Masha said.

Alyona unwrapped the silver paper and stared at the phrase written there. *"Since I first kissed you, my heart was yours completely. I can't live without it. Will you marry me?"*

Alyona couldn't believe the words she had just read. This couldn't be reality. Was she dreaming?

She was speechless. She gazed at Bradley, who noticed her astonishment. He approached her and got down on his knee. He picked up the ring from the little box and gently grabbed her hand. "Will you marry me?"

Alyona stood frozen. For the first time, she realized she wanted to spend the rest of her life with someone, and that someone was Bradley. She felt like the happiest girl in the world. She raised her head and saw her mother crying. Beside her, Masha was gesturing. *"What are you waiting for? Say yes, say yes..."*

With so many emotions clouding Alyona's mind, she began to cry.

Bradley looked at her, confused. "Why are you crying?" he asked. "Did you really think I wasn't going to ask you? I came all the way here for you because I'm desperately in love with you. When I first saw you behind that gate, I knew you were the one I was looking for. I can't let you go."

Alyona wiped away her tears, then looked down at Bradley's hand, which was holding the ring. She smiled. He had chosen the perfect ring for her.

Bradley looked at her impatiently. "So, what do you say?"

"YES! My answer is YES! YES!" Alyona said.

Bradley put the ring on her finger. It fit her perfectly. He got up and kissed her. "Now you're officially mine." He lifted her. Alyona closed her eyes and let herself dream. It was the best day of her life.

Masha and her mother clapped and cheered.

"What a beautiful moment!" Masha said.

"This is more than a beautiful moment. This is something called Love." Her mother said.

"This is a Christmas memory I'll never forget," Masha said, wiping her eyes.

"Now you should think about making a beautiful memory of your own," her mother suggested as she put an arm around Masha's shoulders.

"Ah Mother, I still have time for that."

"There's no time to waste, Masha. Make up your mind. You need to settle down," said her mother.

Masha smiled. "Okay, okay. I'll think about it."

Serafima held her arm. "I know you will. Now, let's go into the kitchen and get the dishes ready for our Christmas lunch."

"Okay, Mother." Masha gazed at Alyona and Bradley one more time. They were kissing and laughing. They made such a perfect couple. Masha wished someone would look at her the way Bradley looked at Alyona. His eyes drank her in. He was crazy about her. Masha sighed and made her way to the kitchen. *"Why doesn't my boyfriend ever look at me that way...?"*

Epilogue

We all want to find that true love that is promised forever. Despite our delusions, we shouldn't give up. Most of us think that finding real love happens only on the silver screen, but guess what? It also happens in real life, just as it did for Alyona. She met Bradley when she wasn't looking for love.

Beautiful things happen when you least expect them. You just have to believe and hope that they will happen to you, too.

THE END

About the Author

Elena Marica is a novelist best known for her first novel, The Truth Behind the Shadow, a classic love story that offer an idealist view of true love. The novel seems to have struck a chord with many people.

Elena writes thrillers and sexy, romantic fictions with a bit of drama that keeps you on the edge.

Follow her on Twitter at @ElenaMarica1, on Instagram at elena.marica_fictions or on Facebook at www.facebook.com/ellenamarica